❧ *Stuck with Luck*

Books by Elizabeth Johnson

THE LITTLE KNIGHT
THE THREE-IN-ONE PRINCE
NO MAGIC, THANK YOU
STUCK WITH LUCK

Weekly Reader Children's Book Club

presents

STUCK WITH LUCK

by Elizabeth Johnson

Illustrated by Trina Schart Hyman

Little, Brown and Company   *Boston   Toronto*

LIBRARY OF CONGRESS CATALOG CARD NO. 67-17548

Published simultaneously in Canada
by Little, Brown & Company (Canada) Limited

PRINTED IN THE UNITED STATES OF AMERICA
WEEKLY READER BOOK CLUB EDITION
INTERMEDIATE DIVISION

❧ *Chapter I*

"SEE A PIN and pick it up, all the day you'll have good luck. See a pin and let it lay, bad luck will haunt you all the day."

Tom Swenson chanted the magic rhyme as he leaned over and picked up a common pin from the sidewalk. Generally pins are not found out of doors. Maybe this one was especially extra lucky.

Tom stopped walking. He looked in back of him, way down to where the sidewalk turned the corner. No one was coming. In front of him there was no one as far ahead as he could see. At his right, the lawn stretched back between the Hartmans' house and the Lindgrens'. Both families were away for the summer. The curtains were all pulled down, making the windows look empty between the frames. Not even a leaf moved. Nobody in sight.

Across the street the Jones house was so far back from the sidewalk it was hard to see if anyone was there. The porch was covered with vine. If someone were sitting there, he could scarcely see where Tom was standing, much less what he was doing. This was a good time to make his usual wish.

He stuck the pin in his shirt pocket. Then he closed his eyes tight, squinching them together so hard that he seemed to see little flashing lights inside them. With his legs crossed and his arms held out to keep his balance, he crossed the second finger over the forefinger on each hand.

"I wish," he said. Then he stopped.

This surely was the best wishing position, especially on a lucky day. Even when he had awakened this morning Tom had felt that this was going to be A DAY. Unfortunately, he could not always count on this feeling. He had had it before. Once it had worked out well. He had found a kitten, without even wishing for it. Of course, his mother had not let him keep it, but the feeling had been good while it lasted.

Today even his elbows seemed to tingle. If he was going to be that lucky he had better be careful how he worded his wish. Terrible things could happen if you got a wrong word in or a right word in the wrong place.

"I wish," he said again slowly.

"Well! Get on with it, will you? I've not got all day to be standing around here with me fingers upraised and a'holding me breath whilst you make up your mind! It's tired that I am of standing here, I can tell you!"

Tom's eyes flew open. Standing before him was a wee

4

man, about two feet high, with flashing dark eyes, a beard that went from ear to ear under his chin, a longish nose, tousled hair and a cross expression. His clothes were very odd. He was holding a red hat in his right hand, while his left was raised in the air. He wore a green coat with wide lapels that stopped right at his waist, a green vest, long green pants and heavy thick-soled shoes that laced halfway up his legs.

Tom stared with his mouth half open, like a fish coming up to bite the bait on a hook.

"Well!" said the wee man again, stamping his right foot. "For what were you wishing?"

"A dog," Tom all but whispered. If tingling elbows were a sign that such a fiery wee man was to appear, maybe tingles were something to avoid.

"As easy as that, eh? You shall have one. How's this?" The wee man lifted his left hand still higher, pointed his forefinger and screwed up his face. Suddenly a large Irish setter jumped on Tom, slobbering all over him with the glee of a lost dog finding its owner.

"No! No!" gasped Tom, half embracing and half pushing away the great red dog. "My mother will *kill* me."

"Your mother will kill you?" sputtered the wee man.

"Now what kind of a mother is that to kill her own son? Or is your family too large — ah, the pity."

"No. I'm the only one, but —"

"But me no buts," snapped the wee man. "I'll protect you. No mother shall kill her son, her only son at that, without Magruder McGillicuddy O'Toole coming to the rescue."

"Ma — what?" said Tom.

"What do you mean, Ma-what. That's me name."

"What kind of a name is that?"

"What kind of a name? And what kind of a name would a fine upstanding leprechaun be having but a good Irish one?"

"You're a leprechaun?" Tom squeaked his excitement.

"And what other creature would be answering a good Irish lad's wish but a leprechaun?" snapped Mr. Magruder McGillicuddy O'Toole.

"Irish? I'm not Irish. I'm Swedish. American really. My grandfather was Swedish."

"Swedish — American? Wurra, wurra. And how did I get into such a mess as this? American I expected since I've come to this country for a wee look around. Swedish, you say?

"Come to think of it, you don't look Irish. No freckles, no red hair, no fine Irish brogue to your tongue. So why would you be summoning me? You must be a blithering idiot!!!" The wee man stuck out his bearded chin and glared at Tom.

In real alarm Tom backed up as much as he could with the Irish setter going round and round his legs, happily whipping them with his big tail.

Magruder McGillicuddy O'Toole shook himself and said, "There, there, lad. Don't be alarmed. 'Tis a testy old leprechaun I am and sometimes I have to talk to myself, else I get out of hand. You'll be excusing me for a minute."

The leprechaun turned his back on Tom and talked to himself, loud enough for Tom to hear. "Now you must watch it, Magruder. Here you are in a strange land and you not knowing the customs and all. Just because someone wished when you happened to be handy by is no reason in the United States of America to be answering the summons. There must be others to do it here. You're not in Ireland now. You should mind your own business entirely . . . .

"But then, Magruder, me boyo, what about this poor lad whose mother is going to kill him?"

"Please," said Tom. "I didn't mean she really would. I just meant she wouldn't like my having a —"

"Don't interrupt where you're not welcome!" snapped Magruder. "Now where was I in me talking to me? Oh yes, what to do about this boy whose mother —" Then he suddenly understood what Tom had been saying. "You say she won't be killing you after all? Now that *is* a relief. So what were you wishing for a dog for, if you knew she wouldn't be liking it? Ah, 'tis a fine dog, that one there."

"I just thought a small dog she might not mind so much. But this one — it's awfully nice, you understand — but it's too big. Could you do a smaller one? Please?" Tom crossed his fingers again to help his luck.

"Well, now to be sure. And don't we have a fine Irish terrier? Just a wee bit of a dog. A bit yippy in bark but a fine dog for all that. Would that suit you — and your mother?"

"Well," said Tom timidly. After all the leprechaun was being very nice again. He didn't want to annoy him. "I had thought maybe a little black Scottie would be nice."

"A SCOTTIE! from a leprechaun!?" The wee man's anger was so great that his voice came out as nothing much more than a hoarse rasp. "Saints preserve us! What kind of a dog is that for a true Irishman to produce? 'Tis an insult, it is! You'll take an Irish terrier or nothing, me boyo. Make up your mind and fast. I can't be wasting my time on such as you. A Scottie, indeed!" Magruder's hair stood out from his head like quills on a porcupine.

"Thank you. An Irish terrier will be fine," said Tom quickly.

Suddenly, in place of the large setter there danced before him a small reddish brown bristle-haired Irish terrier with bright shining eyes and a stubby wagging tail. He jumped on Tom with the same welcoming glee as the large dog had. Tom got down on his knees and hugged him. Holding him close, he crooned, "Oh, thank you, thank you. Hi, Ole, old boy." And he rubbed the dog's ears between his hands.

"Ole? You can't be calling that dog that name. 'Twould turn every one of his brown hairs gray to have to answer to that!"

"But I had always planned to have a dog named Ole. Then it would be like yodeling when I called him. See — Ole, O Ole, O Ole," caroled Tom. The dog cowered to the ground and put his head down so that his paws covered his ears.

"See!" snapped Magruder. " 'Twill never do. 'Tis an

Irish dog you have there. Never forget it. You leave your yodeling to yodelers and give him a good Irish name. Try Patrick or Michael or —" As he said Michael, the dog stood up and wagged his tail. "Now, there's your answer."

"I'll call him Michael — Michael — what did you say your name was — for you, but Mike for short."

"Well, now, well, now. 'Tis Magruder McGillicuddy O'Toole." The leprechaun was pleased and flustered. " 'Tis overcome I am. That's very nice of you. I never had anything named for me before. You're a very nice boy, even if you're not Irish. I think I'll have to fix it so your mother will like Michael McGillicuddy, too."

"Oh, could you? I mean, would you, please?"

The leprechaun closed his eyes for the briefest moment, opened them and said, " 'Tis done. Now I must be on me way."

He raised the hand that was still clutching the red hat, placed it firmly on his head and disappeared instantly.

Tom blinked several times as if he expected to see the little man between blinks.

"Good-bye, sir, and thank you," he called softly, not knowing whether the leprechaun was still within earshot or not.

Then he said, "Come on, Mike. We have to go home and see if Mom really likes you."

Boy and small dog ran down the street toward home with the dog yipping excitedly and Tom calling, "Mom, Mom, look what followed me home!"

That happened at seven minutes past four on a hot Tuesday in July.

❧ *Chapter II*

AT SEVEN MINUTES PAST SIX on the same hot Tuesday in July, Tom was out in his side yard trying to teach Mike to catch a stick and bring it to him. Mike was his dog for sure now.

His mother had laughed when Tom came running in shouting,"Look what followed me home!"

She said, "Followed you, Tommy? He almost beat you here. Isn't he cute? Where did you get him?"

"A man gave him to me," Tom said. It was true. Magruder McGillicuddy O'Toole was a man — of sorts — a wee man, a fairy man, but a man for all that. If Tom had said a leprechaun, his mother would never have believed him. Even now she looked a little doubtful.

"Why should he give him to you?"

"Er — he didn't want him and I did. Oh, please, Mom, please! I'll take all care of him. I'll feed him, walk him, wash him, everything."

"Well, we'll see what your father says when he gets home. If he says it's all right for you to keep him, it'll be all right with me. He certainly is a cute dog. I don't know when I've liked a dog before." She leaned down and scratched behind Mike's ear gently. The dog pushed up to her legs lovingly. Tom could see that some kind of charm was certainly working on his mother.

When Tom's father came home, Mike was at the door to greet him. He barked only once, then danced on his hind legs with his front paws up and his eyes shining.

"Hello, what's this," said Swenson, taking the dog's head in his hands.

"A man gave him to me, Dad. His name is Mike. Mom says I can keep him if you say so." Tom spattered the words out so fast that his father laughed.

"Whoa, slow down there. The man's name is Mike? Your mother says yes to a dog? Unbelievable! Tell me again slowly."

Tom explained that the dog's name was Mike but he was named for the man, too. And yes, his mother liked the dog. No, he didn't know who the man was or where he lived but honest he had said he could have him.

Then Mr. Swenson said, "Well, if your mother is willing, it's fine with me, but you have to train him and care for him. We had better watch the newspaper ads just to be sure no one else claims him. He looks like a good dog. Wonder what kind he is."

"An Irish terrier," said Tom promptly.

"Oh?" said his father and he looked at Tom keenly.

"How do you know?"

"The man said so."

"Yes, I suppose he would know. After supper, I'll look in the paper to see if anyone is advertising for a lost dog. You mustn't be too upset if he belongs to someone else."

Tom nodded calmly. He felt fairly sure that there would be no ad in the paper, but if his father wanted to look for one that was all right with him.

Now, at seven minutes past six, while his father read the newspaper and his mother did the dishes, Tom threw the stick and said, "Fetch, Mike, fetch."

"Psst, boyo, psst! Come here, would you," said a familiar voice.

Tom whirled around but saw no one.

"Over here behind the big tree," hissed the voice. "I don't want anyone to see me."

With Mike at his side, Tom went over to the largest tree in the neighborhood. The children used it for hiding behind but never before to Tom's knowledge had it been used for hiding leprechauns. He walked completely around it and saw nothing. Then he said, "Where are you? I can't even see you."

"Around here, on the side away from the house. Wait, I'll take off me hat."

Tom went around the tree again, and suddenly before

him stood Magruder McGillicuddy O'Toole. The wee man twisted his red hat around and around in his hands. On his face there was a strange simpering look, as if he were trying to smile sweetly. This was a hard thing to do for one who generally wore a frown.

"And how are you, me boyo? And the dog? Now there is a nice dog. And your mother likes him?"

"Oh, yes, and thank you. I called thanks to you but maybe you didn't hear."

"I heard," said Magruder. "I followed you home. Else how would I be knowing where you live? By the bye, where is it you live?"

"Why, right here!"

"Stupid dolt! Of course I know right here, but where is here is all I'm wanting to know."

"Oh, this is 529 Myrtle Street."

"Myrtle Street!! 529!! Ah, was ever a leprechaun so beset as to find such a dense boy! Myrtle Street where — like in Dublin, Donegal? What town is it? I need to get me bearings. I seem to have lost some of me magic powers. 'Tis undoubtedly due to the long trip I've just had. 'Twill come back, of course, but just for now I thought I would ask—"

The leprechaun talked slower and slower. He was almost apologetic as he finished. Here, obviously, was someone not used to asking for favors.

Tom felt sorry for the wee man standing before him. He was a stranger in a foreign land, needing help. Tom Swenson would help him. He would let him live with him. Hadn't he brought him Mike, the one thing he'd wanted more than anything else? Of course, Magruder would have to be invisible except when they were alone in Tom's bedroom. Wonder what leprechauns eat? Would his magic feed him? Think of having someone who could produce things from nowhere living right with you! And someone you were helping so he would be glad to grant your wishes! Now, since he had a dog, what else could a boy possibly want?

"And don't you know where you live?" The voice was once more snapping its impatience. Here was no person to be pitied. This was one who was quick to anger and before whom you didn't stand daydreaming.

"Oh, 'scuse me," stammered Tom. "This is Oak Groves."

"Oak Groves, eh? Strange. When I put on me hat and said 'Me for the United States' and whist here I came, why did I land in Oak Groves, I wonder? 'Tis not an Irish-sounding name. Are there any Irish folk hereabout?"

"Well." Tom rubbed his cheek thoughtfully. "There are some — the Shanahans, the Flynns —"

"No O'Tooles?" snapped Magruder. "Ah well, 'tis just me holidays, no doubt. But I'll have to wait a bit until I get me magic powers back."

"What magic powers?" asked Tom. He sat down on the ground with his legs crossed under him. It was easier to talk to the leprechaun when he was down nearer the height of the wee man.

"What magic powers, indeed! Why all those that any leprechaun has."

"What, for instance?" persisted Tom.

"Well, there's me Passing Poke."

"What's that?"

"Umm. There's a question does it work now. I'll be after trying." The leprechaun raised his left hand and, with his thumb and forefinger in a pinching position, pointed at Tom's left knee.

Zow! A terrible sting made Tom straighten out his leg in a sudden jerk and rub his knee.

"Ow! Wow! That hurt! That's no Passing Poke! That's a Painful Pinch!"

The leprechaun nodded and a wry grin flickered across his face. "Aye. That one still works."

"Then there's me Size Changer." He pointed at a rock at the foot of the tree. Nothing happened to it.

"Alas! Alack! Wurra, wurra. You see. It doesn't work. Nor me Disappearing Digit, I suppose." He raised the little finger of his right hand and pointed it at the same rock. The result was the same. Nothing happened.

"But you can make things appear out of nothing. Look at Mike. And you disappear when you want. Jeepers, if I could do those things I'd think it was super."

"Ah, but you're not supposed to be able to. I am. And 'tis lost. And me Lilt, too."

"Lilt? What's a Lilt?"

"Well, now. 'Tis strange the Lilt. Whilst you have it 'tis scarcely noticing it you are. With it your days are brighter; your nights more glistening. You laugh easily. You even like getting mad. But without it — ah, 'tis Gloom, Gloom, Gloom. There's even a chant about the Lilt: 'Me Lilt; me lovely Lilt; me flimmering, flittering, glimmering, glittering, lovely, lyrical Lilt.'

"I can never go home without me Lilt. They'd not let me back. I'd be one of those gloomy Irishmen who say there's good and bad in every land, but worse and bad in Ireland. Ah me! I must rest somewhere to restore me powers before ever I can go home."

"You could stay with me," said Tom hesitantly. He had almost changed his mind about asking the poor wee man in a strange country to come live with him. He was not sure he wanted to have such a fiery little man, now cross, now friendly, around all the time. It might be a problem.

Problem or not, it was now too late.

"That will be fine," said Magruder briskly. "I'll do just that. Which is your room? I'll meet you there. No point in bothering your father and mother. I'll just be invisible and go in. They need never know. Which room, I said?"

"That window at the back corner," said Tom, pointing. The leprechaun was gone.

Tom walked slowly toward his house. Having a leprechaun on hand was going to take some planning. Sure, he'd read of leprechauns but he had never thought much about them because they were so Irish. It had never occurred to him that he would ever see one. What should he do, now he actually had one?

He called Mike and together they went back across the street and into the house.

"What did he do?" called Mr. Swenson.

Tom jumped. For a minute he thought his father meant what had the leprechaun done. Then he realized that it was Mike his father meant.

"Oh, he fetched a couple of times. I didn't try anything else. We walked a little instead."

"Did you see if he would heel?" asked Mr. Swenson. "Here, boy." He snapped his fingers at Mike to get him to come closer. The dog trotted over to Tom's father and leaned against his legs while his ears were rubbed. This was plainly going to be one of Mike's best parlor tricks. It had worked with Tom's mother and now his father was certainly enjoying it as much as the little dog.

Tom leaned against the wall beside the door in the living room. He wanted to rush upstairs to see if Mr. Magruder McGillicuddy O'Toole had found the right room and also to see what the leprechaun was up to. But his parents would think that something was wrong with him if he should say, this early in the evening, "Guess I'll go upstairs now."

Wasn't he always the one who protested about being sent upstairs, no matter how late it was? They'd probably try to take his temperature or some silly thing. If they had had a whole bunch of kids in the family, he could sneak off and never be noticed. When you were the only one it was noticed if you went off alone.

His mother came to his rescue by saying, as she came in from the kitchen, "Where are we going to have your dog sleep, Tommy?"

"In my room, please," pleaded Tom. He was so anxious for Mike to sleep in his room that he again ignored the fact that his mother called him Tommy instead of Tom. This was a long battle he was waging — not to be called Tommy, but first things first. A boy had to have his dog sleep with him.

"Well, I don't know," said Mrs. Swenson. "Do you think it is healthy?"

Mr. Swenson laughed. "Oh, Martha, healthy? Every boy should have his dog sleep with him."

Tom jumped. The very words he had been thinking came out of his father's mouth. Was the leprechaun at work?

Mrs. Swenson smiled, sighed a little and said, "I could have said the words for you. I knew you'd say it. See?" She produced a small old rag rug which she had been holding behind her back.

"Why don't you take this up and find a place for him —
not on the bed. If we let you have him in your room, you
must keep him off the bed. Bargain?"

"Bargain!" yelled Tom. "Gee, Mom, thanks. I'll go see
where is best right now. C'mon, Mike."

Boy and dog clattered up the stairs, skittered down the
corridor and slid together through the doorway into Tom's
room.

Mr. and Mrs. Swenson cringed slightly at the noise. As
she sat down and picked up her book Mrs. Swenson said,
"It seems to me we have a new member in the family."

Not just one new member. There were two.

❧ *Chapter III*

IN HIS ROOM, Tom stood stock-still and looked around almost fearfully. Nothing was different. Maybe the leprechaun had decided to move on. But look, there was Mike leaning against the armchair as if his ears were being rubbed. Tom went over and felt gingerly along the arms of the chair. Nothing. He poked at the pillows in the back.

"Stop that!" rasped *the* voice. "Do you want to be poking out me eyes?"

"But, Mr. O'Toole, how am I going to manage if I can't see you? How will I know where you are?"

"You'll know where I am when I need you to know," said the leprechaun in a huff. "Aside from that, just don't go sitting down sudden anywhere at all, at all. I get a little tempery if I get squashed. There's no telling what I'd do if you startled me and sat upon me. No telling. No telling."

"Well, what about me? Whose room is this anyway?"

"Now, hoity toity, none of that!" Mr. O'Toole had

snatched off his hat. There he was lying in the chair leaning way down to scratch Mike's ears. "Don't you get insolent with me, you young whippersnapper. You're nothing but a mere human child. I could do anything to you — when I get back me full powers, that is."

"Does the rug fit?" called Mr. Swenson from down-stairs.

The leprechaun disappeared.

Tom quickly took the rug and placed it on the floor right beside his bed. Mike immediately got to his feet and walked over to it. He sniffed the rug all over, got on it, turned around twice and sank down on it as if it were the

most comfortable place in the whole wide world. There he lay with his head on his forepaws, his eyes watching everything and anything that went on.

"It's fine," called Tom. To his dismay he heard his father's footsteps in the hall. Then he was standing in the doorway.

Mr. Swenson laughed when he saw where the rug was. "A bargain's a bargain! It's not *on* the bed, you're right, but it couldn't be much closer."

He walked in slowly, looking around. "You know, this is a pretty nice room you have here." Calmly he went over to the armchair and sat down.

Tom clapped his hands over his ears, expecting to hear a loud explosion. Nothing happened.

Mr. Swenson grinned at his son. "Hey, I'm not that heavy! Most chairs hold me. You don't have to block your ears in case of a crash. Just for that, while you're up here, why don't you neat up that mess of junk in the corner. Then you come on down and I'll beat you at checkers."

"Sure, fine," said Tom.

His father got up and left, giving Tom a friendly push in the direction of the corner where toys and models, books, papers and pictures were piled up every which way. The push was not hard enough to make Tom work. It just spun him around.

As soon as Mr. Swenson was out of the room, Tom threw himself down onto his bed in relief that nothing had happened while his father was there. But at the same moment that he landed on the bed he felt a strong shove on his stomach as if someone had pushed very hard against it with a pair of feet. The next thing he knew he was rolling over on the floor and an angry voice was saying:

"I told you not to be doing anything suddenlike!" There was the leprechaun, with his red hat in his hand, on his hands and knees looking down from the bed at Tom.

"You said not to *sit* sudden," said Tom, on his back on the floor.

"Sit, lie, just don't be *sudden,*" snapped the leprechaun.

"How come my dad could sit where you were and you didn't kick him off?"

"He gave me time to get out of the way," said Mr. Magruder McGillicuddy O'Toole. "Now clear out that corner of the shelves just as your father said, so I'll have a place to rest me poor weary head without fearing someone will sit on it. I've had a long tiring day and it's a rest I'm needing. Get to it."

Tom rose slowly. He was not too happy. Having a leprechaun — up to now and except for Mike — was really just a pain in the neck.

Even so, he went over to the shelves and began shoving things about, hoping that by pushing a little here, a little there, some kind of order would appear.

"Now, just a minute, me lad." There was Mr. O'Toole walking gingerly over the piles on the shelves. "Surely you can throw away all those broken bits of whatever they are."

"They were cowboys and Indians. I was going to mend them with special glue — when I got the glue."

"Out with them. OUT!" said O'Toole.

Into the wastebasket went headless cowboys and horseless Indians.

"Now that's more like it. What's in these boxes?"

"Well, nothing now, but they'd be good if I ever saved anything."

"OUT! OUT!" snapped the leprechaun.

By now Tom was just mad enough so he threw into the wastebasket all the boxes he had been saving — in case he ever needed them. He threw out papers he had brought home from school. There were some with stars because they were good. (Not too many of those.) There were others with

C's and D's he had been supposed to show his parents, but — somehow had never found quite the right moment. He threw out the odd bits from a broken train track, also the freight cars that had lost their wheels.

All at once there was quite a bit of room on top of the shelf in the corner. He put the books Aunt Ruth had given him down on the second shelf. What was this? Two library books! He snatched one open. It was due July 14. When was that? Tom rushed over to the calendar hanging on the door. Tomorrow. July 14 was tomorrow!

Say, maybe having a leprechaun paid off. He never would have found the books in time to return them to the library without paying a fine. Tomorrow he would do that and look up about leprechauns at the same time. Ha! Maybe he would find out something that would help a poor fellow who had to do everything a leprechaun said.

Tom leaned over to blow dust off the corner shelf. Swoosh. Then he turned and started to say, "There! It's down to the wood." He looked along the shelf. At the end with his red hat still firmly clutched in his hand, sitting with his knees up to his chin and his chin resting on them, sat the wee man. His eyes were half closed as if he were falling asleep.

Tom reached over, thinking to take the red hat so the leprechaun would not drop it if he really fell asleep. Suddenly a small ball of fiery temper was standing before him on the shelf.

"NEVER TOUCH ME HAT!" stormed the leprechaun, glaring at Tom with eyes that flashed sparks of fire.

"I just didn't want you to drop it," stammered Tom. He drew back in such obvious dismay that the leprechaun relaxed a bit.

"Just don't touch me hat," said McGillicuddy again firmly. Then he rose to his feet, looked at the shelf corner and walked over to it, stepping high over a few things like a top, a bag of marbles, a jigsaw puzzle piece that Tom had not noticed in his general clearing up.

When he got to the corner, where the shelves went along the side wall, he said, "Well! Nothing soft for a poor tired traveler to rest his weary bones on?"

"Oh," said Tom. "Here. How about my bathrobe? I never use it anyway." He rushed to his closet, grabbed his bathrobe up off the floor where it had fallen days ago, and scurried back to the corner before the leprechaun could get angry again.

Tom made a rather messy nest of his bathrobe. Wearily

and with great dignity the leprechaun stepped into the center of it, curled down inside it, put on his hat and disappeared.

Tom watched, fascinated. Suddenly he realized he was not seeing the little man any more.

"G'night," he said softly. He tiptoed out of the room to go downstairs and play checkers with his father. Tomorrow he would worry about what he was going to do with one Magruder McGillicuddy O'Toole.

❧ *Chapter IV*

THE NEXT MORNING promptly at nine Tom picked up his library books and gave a hasty look around his room. His bed was made after his own fashion — one quick smoothing of the bottom sheet, a flipping up of the top sheet and blanket and then a push and shove of the spread. There were days when school seemed almost like a good idea, because on school days he didn't have to make his bed.

After last night's clearing up, his room really looked quite neat. He tiptoed over to the nest that his bathrobe made. For the life of him he could not tell whether the leprechaun was there or not. If he was there, was he awake? Not one sound or sight of him had there been all morning. If it weren't for Mike, who was constantly at his side and who had slept beside his bed peacefully all night, Tom might think he had dreamed that he had ever even seen a leprechaun. First thing at the library he would find out about leprechauns. Then, in case Mr. Magruder McGillicuddy O'Toole did return, Tom Swenson would know what to do with him.

Tom plunged down the stairs at his usual wall-shattering speed. He called to his mother as he reached the bottom stair.

"I'm going to the library, Mom."

Mrs. Swenson came from the kitchen wiping her hands on her apron. "That's right. I'd forgotten you had library books. Oh dear, they are probably overdue again. How much money do you need?"

"They are not overdue. They are due *today*," said Tom cockily.

"Today? Will wonders never cease! My, you are lucky to have found them in time."

"Yeah! I'm stuck with luck," grinned Tom. "C'mon, Mike." He held open the screen door for the dog to go out, then giving it an extra push he bounded out and the door slammed shut.

"Oops, sorry!" called Tom as he galloped down the walk.

"Try getting stuck with a little quiet instead of just luck," called his mother as she turned and went back to her work in the kitchen.

At the library steps Tom leaned over and took Mike's

head in both his hands. "Now, Mike, you have to be quiet in here or they won't let you stay. If there's any other dog in there, don't look at him. If you'll stay right with me, you can come in. O.K.?"

Mike pulled his head out of Tom's hands almost as if he were nodding yes.

"Good morning, Tom," said Mrs. Smith, the librarian, as Tom put his books on the main desk. "Is that your dog?"

"Yes, ma'am. A man gave him to me yesterday. His name is Mike."

Mike happily wagged his stub of a tail and all but smiled to be the center of attention.

"How nice. How old is he? He doesn't look like a puppy."

"I don't know. He didn't say." Tom looked at Mike with new attention. If ever he saw Mr. O'Toole again, he would ask him. A boy should know how old his dog is.

"Say, Mrs. Smith, do you have anything that tells about leprechauns? I don't mean stories. I mean facts."

"Why don't you look and see what it says in one of the encyclopedias? You know, they are over there in the corner. Tell me if you need any help. You have read *The Enchanted Schoolhouse*, haven't you?"

"I've read that. It was funny — a leprechaun in Maine. I just wondered if they are all supposed to be alike. The leprechaun in that book is so different from —"

"That's right. The one in *The Hungry Leprechaun*, for instance, is quite different."

Good. Let her think he meant a leprechaun in a book. Anyone would think he was daffy if he had said that he knew a leprechaun. Well, maybe "knew" was not the word, but even if he had said that he had seen one.

The gang would consider him nutty. It was really a good

thing that they were all away on vacation. What if one of them had been around yesterday right after he had received Mike. Boy! Would he ever have been in trouble trying to explain that!

By now Tom was at the shelves where the encyclopedias were. He found the volume he wanted, went over to a table, sat down and started looking. How did you spell it anyway? L-E-P-R-A? O? E?

While he hesitated, the pages of the big book flipped over without his help, to where the word *Leprechaun* stood out in dark type.

"You don't spell very well, do you?" whispered a voice right in front of him, as if someone about two feet tall was standing on the table. "Let's see what it says. To think I'm in an encyclopedia!!"

"You've been here all the time? You can read?" Tom started to speak out loud because he was so surprised to find the leprechaun there. A quick look at Mrs. Smith, who glanced over his way, made him drop his voice until the word "read" was the merest whisper.

"Of course I can read, and why not? 'Tis full of magic I am. You put a lot of words together and they say something.

Isn't that magic, too? Enough of this blathering. Let's see what it says about us fine leprechauns."

The leprechaun, now visible, leaned over the book. The article in the *World Book Encyclopedia* said: "Leprechauns made shoes for the *shees* or fairies of Ireland. These wrinkled little old men were rich and very cranky. They lived alone, far from the towns. People often tried to catch a leprechaun. When captured, the dwarf would try to buy his freedom by telling where he had hidden his pot of gold. But he always tried to escape without paying. People never believed what a leprechaun said."

"Why that's an insult and a blasphemous lie. I'll not have

it!" Where the definition had been there was now a blank space.

"Hey, you put that back," whispered Tom desperately. "You can't do that!"

"What do you mean I can't. Didn't I just? Me Disappearing Digit is back!" There was a taunting teasing note in the leprechaun's whisper. There was glee, too, because his magic had been restored.

"Escape without paying, not to be believed? How dare they?"

"You just proved you're a crook by taking the words. Please, Mr. O'Toole, the librarian will kill me if she sees what you have done. You're not supposed to ruin library books in this country!"

"Kill you, it is! I never knew a lad who had so many people going to kill him as you have. I didn't ruin the book. I just took out the dreadful lie."

"Look! She's coming over. Oh, put it back!"

The leprechaun disappeared. Mrs. Smith approached the table and said, "Did you find it all right, Tom? You have me interested, too. May I see what it says?" She reached for the book, leaning over Tom's shoulder, to read it flat on the table.

Tom glanced down fearfully. To his great relief there were once more words where the blank space had been.

Together Tom and Mrs. Smith read: "Leprechauns made shoes for the *shees* or fairies of Ireland. These handsome little old men were rich and very pleasant. They lived alone, far from the towns. People often tried to catch a leprechaun. When captured the dwarf would try to buy his freedom by telling where he had hidden his pot of gold. He always told the truth but people were never smart enough to find the gold."

Tom quickly covered his mouth with his hand for fear he would show how funny the new words were.

"That's odd," said Mrs. Smith. "I had always thought they were supposed to be tricky little things, not to be trusted. Ow-w! Something stung me!" She grabbed her wrist. "Watch out you don't get stung, Tom. I'll call the janitor and have him see if there are bees in here.

"It's strange. I can't see where it stung me. It left no mark, but it certainly hurt for a minute." She turned and went back to the desk to ring for the janitor.

"You cut that out!" whispered Tom. "You're going to get us in trouble!"

"Let her mind her tongue then," was the answer. "Now

let's be having a look around. I think I'd like a book on me dear old Ireland."

A book disappeared from the middle of a shelf.

"Put it back!" moaned Tom. "I'll take it out for you. You have to have it stamped out. You can't just take things!"

The book was back on the shelf, upside down to be sure, but where it had been.

"Such a lot of fuss and bother you humans go through," said the leprechaun. "Let me see if there are any pictures."

Tom went over and took the book from the shelf, came back to the table and sat down to look at it. There were lovely colored pictures. He turned a page, but it flipped back.

"Wait!" grumbled the leprechaun. "I've not done looking. Ah, the beauty of that country. I'll look no more. Put it back, lad."

Maybe if he looked at it enough, it would make him want to go back to his country. Tom tucked the book under his arm and said:

"You'll like it when you read it at home. C'mon, we're going. C'mon, Mike," to the dog who had been lying under the table fast asleep.

They stopped at the desk, boy, dog and somewhere one

unseen leprechaun. Tom said, "I think I'll just take this one."

"On Ireland? My, you certainly are feeling full of Irish lore today, aren't you? First leprechauns and now these lovely pictures of Ireland. Looking for a little of the luck of the Irish?"

"Gee, no," sighed Tom. "I've all the luck I can use right now. G'bye, and thanks."

He left the library, remembering to close the door quietly and slowly in case a leprechaun was nearby.

☙ *Chapter V*

Tom walked home from the library. At those moments when no one was approaching him on the sidewalk he kept calling softly.

"Hey, are you there? Hey, Mr. O'Toole, where are you?"

If anyone came toward him, he would stop calling and pretend to be talking to Mike.

"Hey, heel, boy. Hey, sit, boy. Hey, go, boy!" Poor Mike finally became so completely confused by the orders that he ignored Tom entirely and happily sniffed his way home.

As they went up the front walk Tom had a good idea. If he took his bike and his lunch and the picture book about Ireland, maybe the leprechaun would come on a picnic, too. He seemed to like to travel. Then maybe, just maybe, there would be a way to make him decide to go home. Anyway, Mike would come and ride in the basket on the handlebars and get to know the countryside.

"Hey, Mom," called Tom as he went in the house. Just

in time he remembered to stick his foot back and catch the door on his heel before it slammed shut. He cringed a bit, expecting to be hit or stung — if a leprechaun had not moved as fast as the door. Nothing happened. Phew! what a relief!

"Mom, could I have a sandwich and take Mike on my bike out to the park?"

"That's a good idea, Tommy. It's lonely for you here with all the boys gone. Dad was sorry he couldn't get away, too."

"Oh, that's O.K. Now that I have Mike. And, Mom, it's Tom, remember?"

Mrs. Swenson smiled. "I know. And sometimes I really do remember. You're proving you've grown up by being able to be by yourself so well. I guess I should try harder to use your right name. Go get your bike out of the garage and I'll fix your lunch."

By himself, indeed! The trouble was he didn't know when he was by himself or when someone named Magruder McGillicuddy O'Toole was at hand.

" 'Tis a fine idea you have there, lad. I think I'll come along, too, and have a look." Tom wished he didn't jump every time *the* voice sounded, but all he said was, "Good!"

He wheeled the bike up to the back steps and leaned it

against the railing. As he ran up the steps to get his lunch he thought, "Ha! it's working!"

He picked up his book, tucked it under his arm, scooped up Mike to carry him down and put him in the basket.

Mrs. Swenson finished putting a sandwich and some cookies in a paper bag.

"Can you carry this, too? I'd better take it out for you."

Just then the telephone rang. "Oh dear," she said. "Here, grab the bag with your fingers. There. Be careful, dear, and be back by five." Off she hurried to answer the telephone.

Luckily the back screen door was not latched so Tom backed against it and with dog, book and lunch staggered down the steps and dumped all three in the basket.

With a piercing yelp Mike was up and out of the basket, scrabbling down the front wheel to the ground. There he turned and barked furiously at the basket.

Mr. O'Toole was standing in the corner of the basket, waving his arms. "There's not room for him and me," he insisted. "He'll be walking all over me. I'll not have it. How would you like it if a great furry thing were suddenly dumped on you?"

As soon as Mike saw Mr. O'Toole in the basket he stopped barking and wagged his tail.

"There'd be room if you would just show where you are. Mike doesn't step on anyone he sees. Wait, I'll get my sweater; then no one else will see you."

Tom rushed up the steps to the back entry, grabbed his old green sweater that was hanging there. Letting the door slam, he clomped down the steps once more, jumped on his bike and off they went down the driveway and out to the street.

Mrs. Swenson, talking on the telephone, said to her friend, "My quiet son, whose name is Tom, not Tommy, has just left on a picnic all by himself."

With his bicycle basket really full of dog, lunch, book and leprechaun, Tom pedaled out from town toward the park. There woodlands, benches, picnic areas and fireplaces had been set up by Oak Groves to give its residents a place to picnic. There were large areas for groups, small ones if you were all by yourself as Tom planned to be. At least that is the way it would look.

On the way, Tom explained the sights to Mike. The dog sat with panting tongue enjoying every minute of it.

"There's where Joey Gould lives. You'll like him; he likes dogs. Over there is where Jim Cordello lives. He's nice

and he can't help it if his sister has a cat. Some dogs like cats. Maybe you do."

"No true Irish terrier ever liked a cat," said *the* voice. Mr. Magruder McGillicuddy O'Toole stuck his head out from under the sweater that was covering him from public view. He glared at Tom.

"How old is Mike?" asked Tom quickly, remembering his promise to himself to find out.

"Let me see," said the Leprechaun, grasping his chin with one hand while the other held his hat. "He must be close onto — whyever did you want to know?"

"Well, I just thought when anyone asked me I could tell them how old he is."

"Oh — well — tell them three."

"Three what?"

"Years, decades, centuries. Who's to know? Just say three. 'Twill do, you'll see."

"Mr. O'Toole, now that you're talking and I can see you could I ask you something?"

"There's no harm in asking, me lad — and no proof in answering. What do you want to know? I'm in a gentle mood, me boyo. Ask me."

The leprechaun leaned back comfortably in the corner of the basket. His knees were up and his feet firmly planted on the floor of the basket so he would not slip about with the motion. He crossed one leg over the other, put his hat on the knee that was sticking up and clasped his hands in back of his head.

He looked so small, mild and even friendly that Tom, to his own surprise, suddenly reached forward and teasingly grabbed the hat. Holding it high in the air with his right hand while guiding the bike with his left, he asked his question.

"Why am I never to touch this hat?"

The leprechaun sprang up in the basket fast and furiously, all gentleness gone. The front wheel wobbled dangerously. Tom slammed the hat on his own head to grab the handlebars with both hands so the bike would not tip over.

A cold chill went through him. He could see the handlebar, both handlebars, but not his hands on them! He tilted his head down and looked for the rest of himself. He could see the seat of the bike and the pedals going around but nothing of himself. He was completely invisible!

The leprechaun, by now, was almost beside himself with rage. His voice, which was raspy in its normal state, sounded like a buzz saw.

"Give me back me hat. Where are you? Give it me, I say."

Just then as Tom was still pedaling the bike slowly, enjoying and yet shivering a little at this state of not being able to be seen, the path turned a curve in the woods. Just ahead, off the path, two people were picnicking. They were sitting back to the path but even so Tom could see trouble if they turned around.

"Wait a minute. Shh." He reached over and tapped the leprechaun on his shoulder. "There are some people. They mustn't see you. Duck down under the sweater until we get past them. Hurry up!"

The leprechaun sat down, facing Tom, pulled the sweater up over him and glared out under it at Tom as if he were trying to will the hat off Tom's head.

The hat! For a minute Tom had forgotten about his own condition. He did not want to take it off. Mr. Magruder McGillicuddy O'Toole might grab it, and Tom would lose his chance to make it work for him. Maybe the two people wouldn't turn around.

Tom pedaled faster, watching them. They'd never notice. They were the mushy kind. The man was lying with his head on the woman's lap as she sat leaning against the tree. He was safe all right.

He would have been safe, except that Mike barked, just once as if to say Hi.

The woman turned her head and looked at the bicycle going by with a dog in the basket. Then she looked back at her friend. Suddenly she jumped. She said, "Dog in the basket. That bike is going all by itself!"

The man said lazily, "It sounded as if you said the bike is going all by itself."

"I did. It is. Sit up and look!"

By now Tom was pedaling as fast as he could down the path to get around the next curve.

The man sat up and looked just in time to see the bike with nobody on it go pedaling around a group of trees out of sight.

"Mmmm. That's odd. There must be a simple explanation for that. I would have said it was impossible if I hadn't seen it with my own eyes. Must be some kid's private invention. Didn't hear any motor, though. After I've had another piece of that delicious cake, we might go look. But

then, who really cares?" He leaned against the tree beside the woman and reached for a piece of cake.

Tom stopped worrying about the two people. He was having his own adventure. He pulled the bike off the path, got off it and walked it quite a way into the woods, where he gently lowered it to the ground so the occupants of the basket could get out easily.

Mike jumped out first, before basket and bike reached the ground. Magruder angrily hung on to the side of the basket until it was on the ground. Then he stood up. Stepping out, with sweater and book, he demanded loudly, "All right, me boyo. All right. That's enough. Give me back me hat!" And he swung about with his arms, hoping to feel where Tom was.

Tom put the bike on its stand and moved off a bit to be sure he wouldn't be found until he was ready. "Aw, now wait a minute, Mr. O'Toole. I'll give it back. Just let me try it for a while. I've never been invisible before. It's fun."

Hearing Tom's voice but not seeing him, Mike began running in frantic circles around the voice. Tom had to jump aside each time the dog came racing past for fear both he and Mike would get hurt if they collided.

"Hey! Wait, Mike! Wait! Don't! Don't!"

This was more to the leprechaun's liking. He sat down calmly leaning against a tree and said, "Give me back me hat, boyo, and you won't be after having all that trouble."

Tom finally swung himself up onto a low branch of another tree so he could catch his breath and decide what to do. Mike, having lost Tom completely, trotted off through the trees.

Tom did not really want to be invisible, certainly not all the time and probably not often. It was interesting for a time though. He held out his right hand and looked at it. Not one sign of it could he see. He put his hands together. Say, this really was invisibility. He could feel either hand but he could not see them.

What could he do with this new state of being unseen? Nobody was around for him to startle. He certainly was not going near Mr. O'Toole when he was so angry. With Mike thrown off his trail maybe he could explore a bit without dog or leprechaun knowing where he was.

Quietly he swung down from the branch of the tree and started toward the next tree, where a swing was hanging. Crack! went a stick under his foot.

Instantly the leprechaun was on his feet glaring in Tom's

direction. Tom grinned to himself. He was safe from Passing Pokes as long as he could not be seen.

It was hard to avoid stepping on sticks when he could not see exactly where his foot was going to land. He tiptoed, placing each foot carefully in clear spots where no twigs seemed to be.

He reached the swing and sat down upon it. Whoops! This was a mistake. The leprechaun could tell where he was by the motion of the swing. Tom hopped off, grabbed the seat and held it straight as if someone were sitting on it. Then, walking backward, still holding the board, he raised it as high in the air as he could and gave it a mighty push.

The board sailed through the air, reached the end of the swing, came back and then forward again. Tom was pleased it was going so smoothly. It looked as if he were playing the game of letting the old cat die. Would it fool the leprechaun?

Sure enough, it did. There was Magruder McGillicuddy O'Toole standing on the ground wagging his chin angrily and using his pinching motion with both hands, following the swing up and back, up and back.

Tom thought of saying "Ow" just for fun. However, he remembered just in time that the sound of his voice would give away exactly where he was standing.

In a minute the leprechaun realized that the swing was going all by itself.

"All right for you, me boyo. Give me back me hat. 'Twill be great trouble you are in if you don't."

Pooh! What could the leprechaun do? Hadn't Tom already fooled him with the swing? Now, let's see, what could Tom do next?

He ran, jumped over a bench, swung on a branch, clambered up a tree and down again. He looked around. What now? That was the trouble. There was really nothing to do here in a deserted picnic area. If he were downtown in the stores or even at home, being invisible would be much more fun. But it was too far to walk, and if he got on his bike the leprechaun would have him for sure.

Suddenly he did not want to be invisible any more.

He reached up and took off the hat. There it was, bright red in his hand. But his hand *did not show!*

"Hey!" Tom's voice was a screech of fright. "Hey! I have it off and I'm still invisible. Mr. O'Toole, help! What do I do?"

He looked at the leprechaun, who was sitting on the ground once more, leaning against his tree with the sweater beside him and the book in his lap. He looked like a leprechaun completely in charge of all he surveyed.

"Me magic powers are all restored," he said smugly, and grinned at Tom. "Now, if you'll be so kind as to return me hat, I'll be after making you be seen again."

"I thought it was the hat that made you invisible."

"Did you now? Now maybe you'll be knowing there's more to being a leprechaun than having a hat."

The words in the encyclopedia flashed through Tom's mind: "People never believed what a leprechaun said."

What if Mr. O'Toole took back the hat and then did not make Tom visible. What would he do then?

"Give me me hat." The words were beginning to sound like a chant in themselves.

"I'm sorry, Mr. O'Toole," said Tom bravely. "But first you have to make me visible — entirely seeable — then I'll give you the hat."

"We could do it at the same time," said O'Toole slyly.

"No. First me, then the hat."

"What a lot of blather for a little thing. There you are." Suddenly Tom was there, all of him, even to his tiniest fingernail.

"Oh boy, thanks!" Tom ran over and with great relief gave the hat to Mr. O'Toole.

❧ *Chapter VI*

Tom was ravenously hungry. The strain of being invisible certainly had given him a good appetite. He thought he would probably die of starvation right then and there if he didn't have something to eat immediately.

He whistled for Mike to come and turned to go to the bike to get his lunch from the basket. As he did so he heard or felt a loud noise, like a clap of thunder, but as if it were inside him. It whanged the way an elastic band breaks when pulled just too far, or the way the whole line collapses in tug of war when the other side lets go. Tom fell down with the force of the clap.

As he started to get up he realized he had become very small. He stood all the way up and there was the leprechaun standing in front of him. They were just the same size!

Tom gasped and the leprechaun said, "Ha! Let this be a lesson to you. I told you never touch me hat."

"But I gave it back," wailed Tom.

"Stop your sniveling! I'm just seeing for sure if all me powers are back. And I'm having me a bit of revenge. Nobody tricks a leprechaun without paying for it. You try this size for a while. Go off and leave me be whilst I look at these beauteous pictures of me dear old Ireland."

Mike came over and sniffed at Tom in a puzzled sort of way. The dog seemed enormous. His head was even higher than Tom's. After a minute Mike turned and crept under a bush as if to get away from it all.

Well, small or not, Tom still had his great hunger. He

started once more for his bike. It was not easy walking when you were so little. No wonder babies had trouble. Just to get over the root of the tree took a lot of effort. He was so busy working on his walking that it did not occur to him what he would have another problem when he got to the bike.

His lunch was in the basket — way up high in the basket. Why had he bothered to put the bike on its stand? It would have been easier actually to have left it lying on the ground. But no, good old do-it-the-hard-way Swenson, he had to leave it standing up.

The leprechaun had been able to get into the basket by himself. How had he done it? Tom reached up and pulled the pedal on his side so it was as far down as it could be while the other pedal was way up on the far side. Then, hanging on to the lower structure of the bike with both hands, he tried lifting his foot up to the pedal. Maybe if he stood on that it would make him tall enough to reach into the basket.

A titter behind him told him that the leprechaun was enjoying his revenge. This made Tom mad. All right. He'd show him! He wouldn't bother with his lunch. We-ell, just one quick try.

He could not raise his foot up high enough to reach the pedal. He finally managed to get his knee on the pedal, but as soon as he put his weight on it the bike began to totter. It certainly would not help matters if the bike fell on him. Tom jumped off. Magruder McGillicuddy O'Toole was peering at him delightedly over the top of the book.

"How did you get into the basket?" asked Tom.

"How do you think? I'm a leprechaun, don't forget. I fly. Now, be off with you, you're disturbing me peace."

Tom walked off dejectedly. Hunger filled him from head to toe. Even though head to toe was not a great distance now, it was empty all the way. It must have been at least five hours since breakfast. And all he had had for breakfast were four pancakes. Just his luck that he had said no at the fifth one. He sure was stuck with luck these days.

He clambered over to a picnic table and benches. Ah, there was a trash barrel. Maybe someone had left some food. But when he got to the barrel he could not even see in. He was too short.

The barrel stood right next to the table. Maybe he could work this out. By throwing himself on his stomach onto the bench he managed to pull himself up so he was on top of the bench. From there he stood up and worked the same way up to the table top. There, triumphantly, he stood up to walk down to the end to see what was in the barrel.

"Watch it, me boyo. People coming. Better hide. Unless, of course, you want them to see you like this," called the leprechaun.

Tom had been so busy getting up on the table that he had not heard any sound. Now he could hear voices mur-

muring in the distance coming closer. He looked over at the leprechaun. He had disappeared. The book was still up as if he were reading it, but no Magruder McGillicuddy O'Toole was in sight.

Tom was desperate. Where should he hide? He was right out in the open on the top of the table. From there, the ground looked as far away as if he were on the top of a three-story building. If he got inside the trash barrel he would never be able to get out.

He flung himself face down on the table, backed to the edge and lowered himself, feet first, to the bench on the side away from the path. Then he did the same thing on the bench. Once on the ground, he scuttled into the near-est bushes.

Around the corner came the same two people strolling along hand in hand. The woman gave a little shriek and exclaimed, "I saw something over there. It moved. Let's go back."

"Don't be silly. There is nothing wild in these woods. Oh, there's that bike. Let's go see."

Tom crawled into the bushes, and then lay flat and very still as he peered out to see what they were going to do. His heart was thumping so, he was sure they would hear it

and come searching for whatever was going thump, thump, thump. What if they found him? How could he explain? His mouth was so dry with fear that it felt as if it were stuffed with cotton. He forgot he had ever been hungry.

Oh, boy, watch out. Here they come.

"See, it *is* some kid. There's his lunch in the basket, his sweater and book on the ground. He must be walking with his dog now. He probably just gave the bike a shove and let it roll ahead of him," said the man as they walked over.

"Look at the book," said the woman. "How do you suppose he got it to stand up like that? It doesn't seem to be touching the ground anywhere. I wonder —" She bent over to look at the book. "Ow-w!" she screamed. "A bee! Kill it! Kill it!"

The man, who had been bending over to examine the bike, straightened up and rushed over to her rescue. He waved his arms around her in the air, saying, "Where, where? I don't see any."

"Oh, I don't know. Let's get out of here," she moaned, sucking the back of her hand where "something" had stung her.

Together the man and woman turned and hurried away down the path to safety. Tom drew a sigh of relief.

He had started to crawl out from under the bushes when a loud whirring sounded over his head. The branches and leaves of the bushes shook and bounced about. Tom fell flat on the ground again, putting his arms over his head.

After a minute, all was still up above, so he lifted his head slowly. He rolled slightly to one side and peered upwards. A large eye was glaring at him, a beady, shining, staring eye. Tom ducked his head down and lay flat.

He held himself as rigid as he possibly could for as long as he could. It seemed like forever. All at once, he heard a twittering sort of sound. A bird! That's all it was. He rolled over onto his back and looked up.

A bluejay was looking down at him. So close was it that Tom could see each feather on the bird's breast. Never had a bird looked so large as this one did now that Tom was small.

Fearing the bird might peck at him with its beak that looked so sharp and menacing, Tom scurried out from under the bushes so fast that he made the bushes shake. This disturbed the bird. With a great fluttering of wings it took off into the air. Strange, he had never realized a bird's wings could make so much noise.

Tom stood up and looked around. The picnic table and

benches blocked his view of the leprechaun. At least he
hoped the leprechaun was still there. What if he had gone!

In panic Tom started to run, forgetting that with his
short legs running was extremely difficult, if not actually
impossible. He promptly tripped over a root and fell face
down. He scrambled to his feet but his left foot slipped into
a hole in the ground. As he tried to catch his balance his
right foot landed in the same place. It was not a large hole,

just large enough for an animal to use as a back tunnel to its burrow down below.

Tom sank into the hole almost up to his hips. There he stuck, wedged in tightly. This was silly. Of course, he could get out. He tried pushing down with his hands on the ground in front of him. It did not work. He tried one hand on either side. No luck. Both hands behind him. Nothing worked.

If he could make the hole larger, he could get one leg out at a time. He tried digging with his hands. Such little hands. Tom looked at them in disgust. If his nails were only a little longer, he could dig better.

Dig? Say, where was Mike? Maybe he could do it.

"Here, Mike. C'mere, old boy. Here, Mike." Tom tried snapping his fingers. Ha! Who could snap anything that little?

Tom whistled. Even in his big days his whistle had not been as good as he would like it to be. Now that he was small, a little scared and quite a bit annoyed, the whistle came out more like steam escaping from a teakettle than any kind of dog-calling whistle. But it worked.

Mike came out from under the bushes. He came over and sniffed Tom front and back. He gave a sort of whimper and stood in front, looking down at him as if wondering what kind of a game Tom was playing.

"Dig, Mike, dig." Tom scratched the dirt with his hands right in front of him. "C'mon, Mike, get it, boy, get it!"

Mike dug furiously with his front paws, making the dirt fly all around him. Then he stopped, cocked his head to one side with ears up, and looked at Tom.

"Good dog. Good dog. Dig some more." Tom dug again. So Mike dug. Every time Mike stopped digging, Tom urged him on. He praised the dog so much that Mike came over and licked Tom's face whenever he stopped. It was plain to see that this digging was not Mike's idea of the most fun in the world, but if this was what Tom wanted, Mike would oblige. Back he would go and dig some more.

After a while Tom was covered with dirt from Mike's digging. It was dirt that had been slobbered around by Mike's kisses. Both boy — leprechaun-size — and dog were hot and panting. Finally, Mike dug enough so Tom could get one leg pulled up. By pushing with his hands, he managed to brace one knee against the side of the tunnel and pull himself up and out onto the ground, where he lay panting and puffing from his hard work.

As he lay catching his breath there was another loud

whang in his ears. What was that? Somebody coming? Where could he hide? He jumped to his feet and stood looking down at Magruder McGillicuddy O'Toole in front of him.

DOWN! He was looking down! He was his own size once more! The relief was so great that Tom sat kerplunk on the picnic bench. His knees felt weak. Look at him, sitting on this thing that had been so hard for him to climb onto when he had been looking for food.

Food! Tom rushed over to the bike, grabbed the sandwich and ran back to the picnic table. With the satisfied air of one who has been through a lot but has finally won, he tore open the sandwich and took a blissful big bite.

❧ *Chapter VII*

TOM FINISHED his sandwich by popping a last large bite into his mouth. He chewed noisily, his mouth partly open. It was a good sandwich but boy, was he ever thirsty now. He had nothing to drink with him and there was no drinking fountain at this particular picnic spot. It seemed as if he could scarcely swallow this last bite.

With a great gulp he got it down, wiped his mouth with the back of his hand, scrunched up the sandwich bag and tossed it into the trash barrel. He was tired from all the strain of being first invisible, then small. And was he thirsty! Suddenly he had a great desire to be with people, not with a leprechaun who had caused him a lot of trouble.

Tom glanced at the leprechaun, who was back sitting against the tree with the book open in front of him. At that moment Mr. O'Toole was looking out over the top of the book as if he were gazing at something far, far away.

He is probably taking stock to see if he has *all* his magic powers restored, Tom thought. Before anything more could happen to him he said, "I'm going back, Mr. O'Toole. I have to return that book to the library. Can I take it now? You can't take it with you."

"Yes, lad, take it. But it's traveling with you I'll be, yet awhile. I'm still missing something. You can carry the book if you want. However, I have the power restored that can put it back on the very shelf from which you took it. But you humans are always wanting to do things by rule so I'll not be interfering. Come on, what's keeping you?"

Before Tom's eyes Magruder McGillicuddy O'Toole rose in the air and landed lightly in the basket of the bicycle still in his sitting position.

"Oh-oh, forgot me sweater," said the leprechaun. The sweater rose in the air and dropped into the basket, half covering the occupant.

"Boy! If I could have done that, maybe I wouldn't have minded being small," thought Tom as he stooped over to pick up the library book that was now lying open on the ground. He walked over to the bike and dropped the book in the basket at the other end from where O'Toole was sitting.

Mike came to the bike to see what was happening. Tom

picked up the dog, who once more seemed to be a small one. He put him in the basket carefully so the leprechaun would not be disturbed. Then Tom snapped up the stand and, swinging himself up onto the bike, pedaled home wearily.

The trip home from the park was uneventful. The leprechaun sat perfectly still staring gloomily ahead. Even Mike scarcely seemed to notice what they were passing. A cat stretched itself on a front porch. Mike looked the other way. A dog barked. Mike seemed slightly startled, but not the least bit interested.

"Thomas Lars Swenson, what have you been up to, to get so dirty in such a short while!" exclaimed Tom's mother. She had just stepped out onto the back porch to hang out a dishtowel when Tom rode down the driveway toward the garage.

"Well, I sort of fell into a hole," said Tom as he hopped off the bike at the back steps and looked up at his mother. A short while, she had said! It seemed like forever. A quick check assured him that the leprechaun had disappeared again.

"Sort of fell? How can you sort of fall? Are you hurt?"

"Nope. I got my foot stuck and Mike helped dig me out."

"Goodness! If they have holes that large for your big feet to get stuck in, they'd better do something to make the park safer. How did it happen?"

"I don't know. Just suddenly there I was." Tom wheeled the bike into the garage.

When he came out, Mrs. Swenson said, "I know it's only half past two, dear, but why don't you go upstairs and clean up."

"Yeah, I guess I will," said Tom. His mother opened her mouth as if to say something and then closed it firmly. She did not want to discourage this willingness to get clean although it certainly surprised her.

Carrying the book and sweater, Tom went in through the back door. He hung his sweater back on the hook. At that Mrs. Swenson could not keep still any longer.

"Tom," she said. "Come here a minute."

He turned toward her. She reached out quickly and felt his forehead the way mothers do when testing for fever.

"Aw, Mom." Tom grinned and ducked away. "Can I help it if I'm just naturally neat?"

"I'll try to remember that." Mrs. Swenson laughed. "Now go get naturally clean, will you? Maybe you have a fever but I can't feel it under all that. Quick! Before you get my kitchen dirty. Throw everything in the wash and you in the tub."

The tub? At two-thirty? Well, maybe it would feel good. Gee, maybe he was coming down with something. Leprechaunitis probably. Feeling better because of his own joke, Tom went upstairs to take a bath at two-thirty of an afternoon!

When he came back to his room, dressed in the clean

clothes his mother had given him, he found that she had taken away his dirty clothes and hung up his bathrobe in the closet. Oh! Oh! That could make trouble. No nest for the leprechaun.

Tom grabbed the cushion that was in the armchair and put it in the corner of the shelves where the bathrobe had been. Pushing it down in the center to make a sort of nest, he called cautiously and softly, "O.K.? Mr. O'Toole?"

"It makes me no never mind," said a gloomy voice. There was Magruder McGillicuddy O'Toole with his hat in his hand walking toward the pillow across the shelf. He sat unhappily on the cushion, crossed his legs under him and rocked back and forth, sighing lustily with each rocking motion.

"What's the matter? You sick?" Tom knelt in the chair and peered at the little man on the shelf. Maybe somebody should feel *his* forehead.

"No. 'Tis me lost Lilt. All me other powers restored, but I'm liltless entirely. You have to have a Lilt to be a true leprechaun. They'll not take me back. Without the Lilt I'll wither up and blow away. Ah, wurra, wurra. I might just as well stay right here until I do."

"Aw, now wait," said Tom. "With all those things you

can do! Look at Mike. Look what you did to me! What more do you need?"

"I told you. I need me Lilt," the leprechaun growled at Tom.

Here was a real problem. If this cross little man was going to stay around all the time it would sure be a mess. Tom would have to think of some way to get rid of him. Obviously the wee man was not up to thinking about anything except how unhappy he was. Once Tom had been like that, only once. Say, maybe, just maybe —

"Do you know what I think?" said Tom.

No answer.

"Well, don't you want to know what I think?"

"Not particularly," said Gloomy O'Toole.

"You're homesick, that's all," said Tom. "I was homesick once at my grandmother's. Boy, was it ever awful. I couldn't eat, 'cause I always had a lump in my throat. I couldn't do anything because all I could think of was how awful I felt. But I wasn't sick. As soon as I got home, I was all right again. Why don't you just go home and see? I'll bet your Lilt's right over there all the time."

The leprechaun cocked his head and looked at Tom thoughtfully.

"You think so now? I've never been out of Ireland before. It could be that the Lilt stays behind. I never thought to ask. I'll have me a try at going back. 'Twas those pictures that did it. If this is homesickness, I'll be having none of it. You know, lad, you may be right. I feel better already just for thinking of going back. Leprechauns belong only in Ireland, I'm thinking."

The leprechaun stood up abruptly, brushed off his coat lapels to spruce himself up. Obviously he was getting ready to go on a trip.

Tom had a horrid thought. What about Mike?

"I can keep Mike, can't I?" He jumped from the chair. Running across the room he knelt beside Mike who was sleeping on his rug. If necessary Tom would throw himself on top of the dog to prevent his disappearance.

"I *gave* him to you, didn't I? Of course you may keep him. And if I find you are right about me Lilt, I'll give you something else, too."

"You will? What?"

"How would you be liking a pot of gold? Mostly that's what humans want from us leprechauns."

"Gee, a pot of gold. Wow! Thanks!"

"If I'm not right back, it means I've found me Lilt, me flimmering, flittering, glimmering, glittering, lovely, lyrical Lilt. You'll find the pot of gold under the big tree out there. Me for Ireland now!"

With a wave of his hat, Magruder McGillicuddy O'Toole put it firmly on his head and disappeared. The clock said exactly seven minutes past four.

At seven minutes past six Tom stood under the big tree

leaning on the shovel he had been using all around its base. Every place he had struck the shovel in Mike had come to help dig, too. Nothing had been found. The leprechaun had not come back. Where then was the pot of gold?

Again the words in the encyclopedia came back to him: "People never believed what a leprechaun said," and "He always tried to escape without paying."

So-ho, the book had been right. Well, O'Toole had his

Lilt back and Tom had Mike and that was just about as lucky as you could get.

"What are you doing?" joked Mr. Swenson, as Tom walked back to the house. "Digging for treasure?"

Tom grinned. "Yeah. And you know what? There isn't any there! C'mon, Mike, let's play ball!"